The Kid That Even the Dogs Didn't Like

The Kid That Even the Dogs Didn't Like

STORIES BY

RAY HALLIDAY

MAMMOTH books
DuBois, Pennsylvania

Copyright © 2013 by Ray Halliday

All rights reserved. No part of this book may be reproduced in any manner without written permission from the publisher, except for brief quotations used in reviews or critical articles.

First edition

ISBN: 978-1-59539-034-9
MAMMOTH books
is an imprint of
MAMMOTH press inc.
7 Juniata Street
DuBois, Pennsylvania 15801

www.mammothbooks.org

Cover design & page layout by Jason Enterline
Artwork by Adam McCauley

Production by Offset Paperback Manufacturers, Inc.

ACKNOWLEDGEMENTS

Some of the stories here appeared in different form in these publications:

"Theory of Relativity" in *Story Quarterly*

"North Carolina" in *Pennsylvania English*

"Wax Paper," "New Baltimore Service Area," "Bowling in Jersey," "Right Out of a Machine," "Chunk of Ice," "Fourth," "Furry," "Blind Asian Woman with Dog," "Saliva," "Farted," "New Format," "The Kid That Even the Dogs Didn't Like," and "The Happiest Guy on the Train" in *The Quarterly*

"Rice Krispies and Bananas" and "Scotch Tape" in *The Crescent Review*

"Spot That Mark Made" in *Quarterly West*

"Protest" in *Stolen Island Review*

"Little Cows" in *The Penguin Review*

Thank you to Dani Leone, Carrie Bradley Neves, Diane Weipert, and Mike DeCapite for reading this over.

Carrie Bradley Neves, Steve Hickoff, Dave Kress, Nancy Krygowski, Dani Leone, Mark Morelli, Neno Perrotta, Jonah Winter, and Dom Leone, thank you.

For Mom and Dad

TABLE OF CONTENTS

Chunk of Ice 1
Scotch Tape 2
Fourth. 7
Furry. 9
Right Out of a Machine 12
Theory of Relativity 15
Farted 20
Little Cows 22
North Carolina 27
Holton 37
The Kid That Even the Dogs Didn't Like 39
Rice Pudding 40
Spot That Mark Made 41
Bad, Superman, Bad 44
Bowling in Jersey 47
Saliva. 50
Blinky Asian Kid 53
Wax Paper 54
New Format 56
The Happiest Guy on the Train 59
Rice Krispies and Bananas 61
The Restaurant of the Third Eye 62
Blind Asian Woman with Dog 63
New Baltimore Service Area 67
Flash Cards. 68
Cork 69
Protest. 70
Pepper. 72
Beverage Display Case. 73

CHUNK OF ICE

A van ran over a frozen puddle and a chunk of ice flew up and hit him in the face and he went to sleep for two weeks. After that, he thought he could see into people's souls and he couldn't get the taste of cheese out of his mouth.

When he woke up, he sat straight up in bed, with the wires and diodes still attached. "I taste cheese," he said.

"Oh, my God," the nurse said as she pushed him down again.

"You're shallow," he said.

Later on, his mom came to see him. "Don't you remember me?" she asked.

"You're Tony," he said.

"What do you see in your dreams?" the doctor asked.

"I see cheese flying at my forehead."

"You're confused," the doctor said.

Often he would sit up in bed and say, "I taste cheese," and the nurses would give him pieces of gum to ease his suffering.

"You're shallow," he told them.

One day he had a thermometer up his butt. He turned his head and looked at the thermometer. "My head is cooking," he said. The nurse hit a button and a lot of doctors and nurses came in, but he died anyway.

A bird flew in the window.

"He was a nice guy," one of the nurses said.

"He wasn't like that before," his mom said.

SCOTCH TAPE

John went into the stationery store and when he saw all the pens he felt better. It was cold and windy out. He had been driving around for awhile, looking for a parking space. He drove around the block once, then twice, then three times waiting for someone to leave, to leave him a parking space. But nobody did and he had to park far away which was frustrating because, really, he lived close enough to walk from his house.

But when he finally got inside it was warm and dry, and they had a nice assortment of pens in an appealing display, and John felt much better.

I love pens, he thought.

He was new in town. He had never been in this store before. In the afternoons he would come home from work and think: today I'll go out and look at the new town, I can buy some pens. But the day would come and go and he would get nervous and just stay in watching TV or making food.

For a long time John thought that there were only Bic-type pens, like in the drug stores. Then one day he wandered into an art store and he saw all the different kinds of pens there were: pens in all colors and thicknesses, pens with all different kinds of inks, pens that would write in any position. Sometimes he felt like he shouldn't be looking at or buying these pens. They were for artists, or graphic artists or draftsmen or something. He delivered flowers. He would just draw a square or a circle and then fill it in, or write the names of the things he liked—like *pie*, or *trees*, or *vacation*.

After a while a girl came up to him and said, "Can I help you find something?"

"No, I'm just looking around," he said.

Boy, she's kind of beautiful, he thought. He didn't see her when he came in. Maybe she would be his girlfriend. He felt good.

Then he felt awkward and dumb because he was new in town and didn't know anybody. He didn't have any friends and the girl probably thought it was weird to say "just looking" in a paper store. He didn't know what to do with his hands, so he put them in his pockets. But he thought that with his hands in his pockets they might think he was sneaky, or that he stole something. So he took his hands out of his pockets and walked to the back of the store, where the big envelopes were.

There were two men standing in the aisle near the folders. One of them said: "I just want to know how it got shipped to Milwaukee instead of here. Can you tell me that? Tom, can you?"

The other guy just stood there. And then he said: "I don't know, Bill. All I really know is that I'm tired. I'm just tired."

John looked down the aisle. The girl was taking the plastic wrapper off a bulletin board. She had on a grey sweater, and she kept pushing up the sleeves. She could be my girlfriend, he thought. My new girlfriend. He had had a girlfriend before. But now he had moved away and she wouldn't be his girlfriend any more.

He was standing near the big envelopes and the two guys were still talking, one saying how can we get it back and the other saying I'm tired, I'm tired.

"Can I help you?" It wasn't the girl; it was a skinny man with a mustache and a sweater vest.

"No," John said, startled. "I'm just going to get some big envelopes."

"Ah, good," the man said and walked away.

John took three envelopes because they were inexpensive, and the fattest, blackest magic marker he could find. The guy took his money, putting the stuff in a big brown bag, maybe too big. "Here," the guy said. "I'll put some tape on this so it doesn't blow around in the wind."

John thought this was unusual but nice. "Thanks," he said. He would make friends in this town.

On the way out he looked at the girl through the window, but she wasn't looking back. She was taking stuff out of a big cardboard box.

There was a xeroxing place down the street and John went in because he had an idea. He thought it would be better if his old girlfriend, Gina, was still his girlfriend. He asked the kid behind the counter for a piece of paper. Then he took out his marker and wrote *I LOVE YOU, GINA*. He made thirty-seven copies on fluorescent green paper, one for each time they had made love. She didn't know it, but he had counted.

When he went to put the copies and the marker back into the big brown bag he saw the roll of scotch tape at the bottom. That guy, John thought, he put a roll of scotch tape in my bag. I'll have to go and give it back to him.

He went outside and watched the cars go by, making sounds. Anybody else would keep it, he thought. But maybe the guy is always very dumb. Maybe he's retarded and he's back there right now getting yelled at and crying because he lost the scotch tape. The thought of the guy, all skinny and teary, wiping off his mustache, almost made John feel like crying. He looked down the street at the store and saw a lady walking in.

That's dumb to think that, John thought. He's probably just a guy. He works in a paper store and has lots of scotch tape. They'll probably never even notice that it's gone. And the girl, the girl would think he was stupid or honest. John thought that she wasn't the kind of person to just think about getting ahead and stepping on people on the way up. She probably cared about people and honesty more. She was a good person.

And John was a good person, too. I'm a good person, he thought, a good person and an honest person and I don't care if people in this town laugh at me because I should've kept the tape.

When he looked in through the window, he couldn't see the guy with the sweater vest. But the girl was up at the register talking to someone. She was holding up some folders. She was still talking when John walked up. He reached in the bag and put the tape on the counter.

"You didn't need any?" she asked. The guy she was talking to looked over too.

"What?" John said. "No, see, the guy accidently put that in my bag."

She was looking at him and smiling. He smiled and nodded his head a few times.

She quit smiling and said, "No, that's a free sample. We're giving them out."

John nodded.

"For *free*," the girl said.

"Oh yeah," John said. "That's pretty good." He picked the tape up off the counter and sure enough, it said *FREE SAMPLE* right on it.

"Boy, what an honest person," the girl said as he walked out the door. But to John it sounded like she meant *what a stupid person.*

I'm a jerk, John thought. My first time out in the new town and already I'm a jerk. The back of his neck felt hot. He took the copies and the envelopes and threw them into the first trash barrel he came to. He put the scotch tape and the magic marker in his coat pocket.

I'm just a jerk, he kept thinking as he walked home.

He felt tired, so he filled up the bathtub and got in, setting the marker and the scotch tape on the side of the tub. The hot water felt good after being out in the cold. It's okay, he thought. The next girl I meet, I won't be a jerk.

Then he remembered his car.

FOURTH

Every morning Jimmy Reilly and Ronnie Menard shoot rocks at me at the bus stop. Every afternoon, Betsy Bollinger writes on my hands at the playground. My mom yells at me when I get home. But I let Betsy Bollinger write on my hands because she is pretty-looking. Yesterday, they got Ralph Scalise. They held him down and covered his face with different color magic markers. He had more magic-marker color than face color left. Ralph Scalise stayed in school the whole day, too. I would've asked to go home. I bet if Ralph Scalise wasn't there, they would have done it to me. At lunch Gordie Scherer, Tom McCaffery, and Jimmy Reilly knocked over the bench, and the principal, Mr. Skully, came and gave everybody a nerve pinch like Mr. Spock does on *Star Trek*. I tried to tell them that I went to get a Dixie cup. But Mr. Skully told me to shut up and zapped me. Nobody fainted like on TV. Jimmy Reilly cried and everybody laughed at him, so I was happy. I really did go to get a Dixie cup. Tom McCaffery and Ralph Scalise had an arm wrestle and knocked my milk over on my pants. It looked like I peed, but I didn't. I asked to go home but they wouldn't let me. Mrs. Richards said I should be more careful. Rafael Casiano hit me in the head with an apple. After school, Ted Carr and Ned Flanagan and me stuck Rafael Casiano into the Salvation Army box across the street. Rafael Casiano's such a shrimp he fit in easy, shorter than me even. Ned helped Rafael Casiano out and they chased me and Ted with rocks. Miss Finegan is the only one I like in the fourth grade. She's not really like a teacher because she's more like our age. She's probably only as old as my sister. But my sister's pretty old for a sister. I guess I like Cindy Ruth Johnson a lot, too. Cindy Ruth

Johnson is from South Carolina and has an accent. When I first saw Cindy Ruth Johnson, I thought she had green hair, but I don't know why I thought that. It's really just blond hair. Phil Cittadino says he'll beat me up if I talk to Cindy Ruth Johnson. He's got a little brother that has cancer and his mother was in a car crash. I figure Phil Cittadino has enough problems and don't let him see me talking to Cindy Ruth Johnson. I slept over at Steve Wells's house once and his mother screamed like a maniac at his brother. Steve Wells is the biggest kid in the fourth grade. He chucked me right over a desk. I ripped his shirt on the way over. He's smart, too. He does experiments and lets me and Ned Flanagan help. Steve Wells made ammonia in Ned's hand and I got to blow in red water and make it turn white. A bunch of us had to stay after school and we shot spitballs at the Christmas tree ornaments. Tom McCaffery knocked one off and we have to stay after again. Everyone who's a Catholic goes to church today and the rest of us sit around and shoot spitballs at the Christmas tree ornaments when Miss Finegan isn't looking. I hate doing stuff behind Miss Finegan's back, but what can you do? Jeff Dembowski draws good, but he threw up in the hallway and had to go home before art. He likes the art teacher because they are both Polish. They put kitty litter on the throw-up, but the hallway still smelled like puke. I had to go home once when I threw up and missed a field trip to the fire station. Everybody spits on Neil Adante on the bus ride home but Neil Adante's used to it. Mostly I just shut up, because I'm afraid they'll turn and spit on me. I hate spit worst of all. Ronnie Menard threw Tom McCaffery's notebook out the window and the bus driver makes him sit in the front of the bus now. Ronnie Menard doesn't care because he's closer to Neil Adante that way. Ronnie Menard threw Tom McCaffery's notebook out the window. But they chase me home with rocks.

FURRY

It made him jump. It was one of those things you just barely see out of the corner of your eye—you see it just for a milli-millisecond and you're not sure what it is. It could be anything, including a giant rock coming at your head at a million miles an hour. That's what makes you jump. That's what made him jump when he was driving his car.

So at first all he did was jump and the car swerved a little, but luckily he was the only one on the road. He saw it out of the corner of his eye, moving fast like a ball, no, like an animal, coming right for the car. No, it was like a dog chasing after the tires, except that it wasn't barking. But it was big and scary. Then he was really scared, because it was a cat.

He was coming up to a stop sign, so he was slowing down. And it was a stop sign, so he couldn't speed up and get out of there fast. He had his window down and he was sure, he was absolutely sure that it was going to jump up and come in through his window, hissing, spitting, making ferocious noises and looking like some catlike kind of devil. He'd never seen a cat move so quick. It was wiggling like furry Jell-O. And he knew it was going to come in through his window and scratch his face off. His forehead got hot and he felt like he was going to pass out. It would dig into his eyes. It would eat his brain. He saw himself crawling into the emergency room and writing on a piece of paper: *A cat scratched my face off.*

Life, he thought, is a cruel and unusual thing.

The cat was under the car now. Or had it gone into that garbage over there? No, it was clinging to the chassis of the car, and it was getting ready to jump in.

He sped away from the stop sign, sweating and shaking. He hadn't even come to a complete stop.

He looked back, but he didn't see anything. Where had it gone? Then he knew. It had somehow got in and was behind the seat, claws and teeth ready to go. It was like a cat, only made by the devil.

He pulled over and got out. He stood there and nobody was anywhere on the road. He was all alone with his car with a cat in it. He looked in through the back windows. He saw the backseat. It had a jump rope and a bottle of Pepsi and a pocket dictionary. He didn't see the cat, but he could feel the cat.

This is not fair, he thought. Why did it pick my car? Why aren't there people to help me? He got down and put his head under the car. Dirt, metal, tar.

The cat is on my back! he thought. He scrambled out from under the car with his head still under the car and scratched his neck up. He was reaching and swatting his back where he could get at it.

Then he felt the back of his head, which had some blood on it. It was running down his back. What an idiot I am, he thought, and he would have laughed, but his head hurt too much. He checked under the seats.

He drove to the drugstore. He went in and got some Band-Aids and a bottle of aspirin. He looked at the magazines, but there was nothing interesting. Nothing at all about cats or devils. When he got to the counter, the girl smiled at him.

"Will that be it?" she said.

He nodded. "Do you live around here?" he said.

She waited a moment and then said, "Mm-hm."

He said, "Has anything strange been happening?" And he looked around to see if anyone was there. "Like have you heard in the news or from friends? I mean, anything about animals? That they've been killing people or anything like that?" He shrugged, looked around. "You know, cats maybe."

"I'll have to ask the manager," the girl said, and went to the back of the store.

Ah, the manager will know, he thought.

RIGHT OUT OF A MACHINE

I can feel her up there. I can feel her motion. She's walking back and forth past my window. And then she's just standing, looking down, trying to see through my curtains. To see me lying in my bed. And then she moves again. There's bars on the window, there's no way she can get in. But the thought of her. I lie here, not moving an inch, not making a sound. I'm trying so hard to hear her. But I can't. I can only feel her. Every once in a while, I can hear my heart, or I can hear one of the mice gnawing in the walls. The mice she brought with her.

She's out in the alley between the two houses, waiting for her fifty dollars.

I came home one day and she was on my porch, just sitting there. She looked normal, but without a home, and crazy. I smiled at her and nodded as I came up the stairs. "Hi," I said. It's all I wanted to do, say hi, walk in, never see her again.

Why my porch?

"I'm looking for my father," she said, wiggling her hands over the paper bag she was holding. "He lives here," she said.

She was older than me. She was just older.

"There are no fathers here," I said, and shut the door on her.

She had gotten up and was ready to walk in. There weren't any fathers. There was a college couple on the first floor and waitresses on the second. Then me in the basement.

That night I wondered if she was sleeping on the porch, but mostly I made dinner and went to sleep. I thought about getting her a blanket, but mostly I was sleeping. The next morning, I didn't see her. She wasn't on the porch. I drove to work, worked, and on the way home, I drove into town to go to the bank machine. There she was outside the bank machine. She didn't say anything or look at me. I put my card in the slot and the door buzzed and I got to go inside, and she didn't try to come in. Her face was dirty and I was taller.

When I came out, she said. "Do you have some dollars you can give me?" She held out her bag to me. I couldn't see anything in it. Inside, it just looked black.

She was smart to stand in front of the bank machine like that.

I almost got run over crossing the street.

That night, again, I made dinner: tuna and crackers. I read a comic book I found in the garbage at work. I went to bed. I woke up, but it was still night and I heard voices upstairs. Up on the porch. I can hear stuff on the porch from my room. I heard her voice and one of the waitresses telling her, "You can't stay here, you can't stay here." I heard Mandy or Minda say she would call the police.

I felt better.

The next morning she came out at me from between the two houses. It was just a little misty and she had sparkles of rain in her hair. I walked to my car fast.

That night, I lay in the dark listening for her. I couldn't hear anything, and then I did. I heard a noise like a mouse in the wall, chewing. Chewing his way through the wall, one mouse bite at a time.

I went to the wall and the noise stopped.

That's how she'll do it, I thought. She'll have the mice gnaw their way in and then she'll crawl through. I'll come home to find her sitting on my kitchen floor, eating tuna and crackers, reading my comic book, cackling. There will be mice all over, running around in tuna cans.

I didn't sleep that night, but I found Mouse-Kill in the linen closet. I put it under the sink and behind my record player.

The next day, I saw a dollar in the road. I parked on top of it and felt great. I lay down on the sidewalk and reached under my car. It was a fifty—dry, straight, and crisp. Right out of a machine.

She can't find her father.

I put the money in my pocket.

I'm afraid I'll be too tired to work tomorrow. It's three already. I fall asleep, then wake up. I can hear my heart beating. I can hear the mouse chewing. But it's slower every time I wake up. It must've reached the poison. It'll never make it to my side of the wall. I haven't spent the money. I have this dream. Two arms come crashing through the window above my bed. Glass sparkles in my eyes.

THEORY OF RELATIVITY

I was standing on a bus heading for two new flannel shirts. There was a girl sitting just below me. She had on a red hunting jacket and gold, big-line corduroys. She was reading an insurance form of some kind.

This was my situation: I'm heading for the Friendly Family Center. It takes twenty minutes on the bus, point A to point B. They have a sale on flannel shirts—two for five dollars. I have seven dollars. One dollar for round-trip bus fare and five for the shirts with change left over for taxes and gum. Or a Coke.

I have an ex-wife, sure. One time we were in the Friendly Family Center and I said, "Look, two shirts for—" I don't know, what could shirts have been back then? Three-fifty? At the most? Anyway, "Three-fifty," I said.

And my wife, as was her wont to do, came over and put the cloth between her fingers and moved her fingers back and forth. "We don't want this," she said. "We don't buy shirts here," she said. "This is cheap," she said.

"That's the whole point," I said. "It's cheap, sure. Sure it's cheap." I was by myself now. My wife had gone over near the nylons aisle. "It doesn't cost much," I said. The whole incident took less than a minute.

The point is, now she's my ex-wife, and I can have as many cheap shirts as I want. I have two. I don't have a wife today. I have seven dollars, two shirts and a possible Coke on my horizon.

Let me also tell you that I was never any good at math. And somebody told me Einstein, that Einstein got *D*s in math. Me, I got some *D*s in a lot of things, mostly math.

Now, let me tell you about the girl sitting below me, her situation, and then other things. Like I said, she was reading an insurance form, maybe for a car she didn't have anymore. I liked her hair. It was black and straight and shiny. It looked like you could make something out of it. Maybe a record.

And I thought I could probably, somehow, get to know her. Maybe I could ask her a question—"Are you all right?" Meaning, how was she, mentally and physically, after the accident that took her car.

Mentally and physically, I'm not married.

It might take fifteen seconds or something, to ask her. But I could see it in my head, the future:

Me: Are you all right?

Her: *Harumph.*

Or

Her: What? What do you mean?

So, luckily I didn't ask her. But I wanted to ask her something. A kid was sitting next to her. He had a math book in his hand, but he was looking out the window and eating potato chips. He was pulling them out of the bag and putting them in his mouth absentmindedly and bits of potato chips were falling out of his mouth and onto his math book, *Math: Our Turn*. Einstein, I thought.

I thought *Theory of Relativity*.

And then the bus stopped and the kid got out, and all the potato-chip crumbs fell to the floor and around the girl. I excused myself and wiggled past her and into the seat next to the window. I was right next to her.

I thought of my ex-wife, looking down on this scene, picking up the bus like the Incredible Colossal Ex-Wife, picking up the bus and dumping me out, and making fun of my shirt.

"It's my ex-wife," I would say apologetically.

My ex-wife used to sigh in the morning before I went to work. "You're not wearing that are you?" Or sometimes she would say, "I won't be seen with you dressed like that."

Now I have two shirts. After my wife left, I threw all my shirts onto the road and watched the cars roll over them. Some blew away. Some dogs carried some away. There were nineteen of them, shirts.

Then I threw the pants out. Then I threw all my underwear out, then socks and belts. Then I went for some of the furniture, and then the cops came.

Now I have two shirts and I was going to the FFC to get two more. Don't think I'm getting flamboyant though. The shirt I have on is wearing out. The other one, at home, was destroyed.

Point A to point B takes twenty minutes on the bus, because of traffic. On my bike it might only take fifteen. But both my bike and my shirt were wrecked when a car pulled out of a parking space and ran me over. It's not as bad as it sounds, the bike and the shirt got the worst of it. Me and the pants were okay.

The girl next to me was turning the pages of the insurance form pretty quickly, like she was done reading it and was just looking for a way to fold it up right.

I can say that if she stays on all the way to the FFC, I don't mind twenty minutes next to this girl.

Twenty minutes on the bus. Fifteen on a bike.

But a plane, I thought, would be even faster.

So this is what I said to her: "You know," I said, getting her attention, "I understand the theory of relativity. Einstein," I said, tapping my temple knowingly. She smiled at me like I was crazy.

But I knew I had her because I *did* understand it. It had just come to me—and I knew she could understand it, too. It was simple, you just had to be on a bus going somewhere.

"I just figured it out," I said. "Just like Einstein." I heard he was on a bus too.

"I go to M.I.T.," she said.

"Okay then," I said. "Check this out. I'm going to the Friendly Family Center, right? It'll take me twenty minutes on the bus. But what if I could fly there? Maybe it would only take five minutes—maybe only a minute, even. Or let's say on a plane it would take a second. I don't really know how fast planes go."

"No," she said. "It would take even longer. Where would you take off and land it?" She was with the program now.

"Hang on," I said. "Hang on, don't derail me here. Remember this is the *theory* of relativity. It's a theory. We can't let practical matters like that get in the way."

She nodded.

"But let's say one second on a plane, okay?" I said. "Suppose now, we can take the Concorde, the supersonic transport. It's less than a second now, right?" And I whispered, "Maybe even less than less than a second. What if you could go faster than that, faster than the supersonic transport. You see? Think. That less than less than a second gets even less. That space gets smaller and smaller."

"So?" she said. I couldn't believe she went to M.I.T.

"Don't you see?" I said. "If you go fast enough you can get there at the same time you left. In no time at all." I raised my eyebrows in anticipation of her realization.

She sighed.

"Wait now," I said. "Suppose we can go even faster. Faster, faster," I said. "So that eventually, we can get there before we leave. I leave my house at 1:00. I get to the FFC at 12:59. I already know what's going to happen when I go. I've already done it. I've already had 12:59. Do you see?" I said. "It's the theory of relativity. With it we can see the future. The future of everything." I waited and then I repeated, "Everything."

She nodded, sort of. "You're right," she said. And then the bus stopped and she got off. It was two more stops to the FFC.

If I could've been moving a little faster, I thought, I could've seen that coming.

I can see two shirts on my horizon, possibly a Coke.

I think there's a way to be sure.

FARTED

I was in the Bone Café in Harvard Square, where I get a muffin and a coffee every morning. The place is pretty clean, but I put up with it because I like watching all the people, especially the girls, walk by. Every morning I eat my muffin and drink my coffee by myself and watch people.

Today I was over near the door, watching, eating—there was a pretty Indian girl who was nervous because I kept staring. There was a nervous guy waiting for a date. He was real obvious about it. He walked all around the Bone Café craning his neck, around and around and walked outside of the Bone Café and over to the T stop and then back, craning his neck. There was also a sort of couple sitting in front of me. And I was sort of watching, sort of listening, and I figured they hadn't known each other for very long. They were both being real polite about how they were eating their croissants, and wiping their mouths a lot, and if they had to cough or sniff they did it real timidly.

They were getting to know each other and saying things like "So what year are you?" and "Where did you grow up?" and then they would just nod very quietly when there were holes in the conversation.

And I farted. Not for any mean reason, just because I had to. And it came up around me for a second and it was pretty stinky, maybe the stinkiest in the world.

Anyway, I could tell by the way the wind was blowing that the fart was headed their way—that it was going to swarm around them for a while, stay there for a little bit before it moved on or disappeared.

And I knew what was happening too. I knew that he was sitting there going—*Oh, God, who farted? Oh, God, what if she thinks I farted?* And she was thinking—*Holy cow, I hope that wasn't him,* and *Oh, God, what if he thinks that's me?* But no matter what, I knew that, forever, they would associate each other with that fart, possibly the stinkiest in the world.

And to think, I had been feeling kind of down.

LITTLE COWS

He didn't know what to do. He had never been to New York City before and he was very excited. He looked out the window. He could hear things out the window: cars blowing horns, sirens, jackhammers, people. He was up on the fifteenth floor; he could look down. He could even look up. It was gray out and it looked like it might rain but he thought for a second that that's what the sky looked like in New York City with all the buildings so close. He thought that maybe the rain never hit the ground here. And he thought that if it did, it might not go anywhere. It might just rise up the sides of the buildings and water would come up to the window of the fifteenth floor.

Better bring the raincoat, he thought.

It was morning. His meeting wasn't until later that afternoon. What to do? He wanted to ride the subway and look at buildings, but mostly he just wanted to walk out in the streets. The streets of a city. He had heard about them. They seemed exciting. And they looked that way on the cab ride in; people all over, yelling at the cab driver, looking real busy. Guys on the side of the street, selling stuff.

He went down to the lobby and said hi to the bellman and the bellman waved. Then he went through the doors.

He didn't know what to do. He looked at the sidewalk. He looked at people walking by. He picked a direction and started walking. He saw a lady buy a pair of sunglasses off a card table. The guy said, "Five," and the lady said, "Three," and the guy shrugged and she got them for three. He looked and found a pair that he liked, one that made him look like the lady and a lot of other people he had seen. Actually, he was surprised that he didn't look out of place. He was a businessman even though he was from the country. His suit looked the same. He felt comfortable.

He held a pair out to the guy. The guy was black and had a lot of bandannas tied all over him. "Five," the guy said.

"Three," he said.

The guy shook his head. "Five."

"Three," he said.

"Four," the guy said. Now it was working.

"Three," he said.

"Look," the guy said. "Give me a break. Where you from, anyway?"

"What?" he said. What was this? "Why I'm from that hotel right over there."

"Oh, yeah," the guy said. "Well give me a break, okay. Give me three and get out of here."

Now he was really in New York City.

He bought a hot dog, a button, an antenna, some cassette tapes, and a pretzel. Everything cost three dollars. He walked around like he was a busy man. Like the rest of them. He looked straight up at the buildings and sometimes he bumped people, but everybody bumped everybody. There was one time, though, when he ran smack-dab into an old woman. "Waah," she said. He said he was sorry and she said, "Sheesh."

He just walked and looked and bought. Then he noticed that his feet were getting just a little tired so he started back toward the hotel. He had been very careful not to get lost. He had counted the numbered streets and the left, right, lefts he had made.

Somehow he got a little lost anyway. He knew he wasn't that bad off though. He was only a few streets off. He was almost home. He was noticing smells. He could smell exhaust and leather and pavement and food. And rain. He looked up and it was amazing. The clouds had come in and you couldn't see the tops of the buildings. They just went up and disappeared about a third of the way up. They just faded away like heaven or something. *Whoa*, he thought, *it's amazing.*

He knew a right would take him home, to the hotel anyway. But then to the left he smelled pavement, food (mostly Chinese), exhaust, and home. Real home, not hotel. He smelled the country.

He knew that maybe he was homesick. That he probably didn't smell anything. Still, he felt like walking down that street, even though he was tired, even though it was getting later. Even though it might rain.

But this street was the same. Food places and guys selling stuff. Nobody was selling the country. He saw sunglasses. And then he saw a guy looking into a big cardboard box on a card table and smiling, making little noises into the box.

He went up and smiled at the guy. The guy smiled back. The guy put his hands out to say, Look in the box. Here's what's in the box.

He looked in the box, smiling. He felt like he was home, although he wasn't sure why. He looked in the box and thought *Oh, five kittens.* He thought *Oh, five cows.* He didn't know what he thought.

The guy raised his eyebrows and rubbed his little mustache.

"Those're *cows*," he said to the guy.

"Oh, yeah," the guy said. "*Those're* cows." And the guy looked real excited and laughed: "Ha."

What was this, he thought. *What was this cows?*

"What's going on here?" he said. "What is this? What are these? You can't have these."

"Wave of the future," the guy said. "Wave of the future is little cows. Little pets. Cute as buttons and friendly as all hell."

He just stood there. There were cows in a cardboard box. It was the most horrible thing he had ever seen. They were just wandering around in a cardboard box. A few of them were chewing tiny cuds. Some of them looked up at him: Hello. One of them let out a little Mickey Mouse moo, and he wondered if he was breathing.

"*Why?*" he asked. Then: "*How?*"

The man clapped his hands in delight. "Science, my friend. It is the miracle of science. A guy in Switzerland developed it. And…" He looked around, sneaky. "I have a connection with a guy who smuggled a few 'experimentals' out. Highly illegal, if you know what I mean."

"*But why?*" he said.

"Why?" the guy said like he couldn't believe it. "Why not? Look at these cute little things. They're going to be the next pet sensation. They're adorable. They're the nicest animals on earth. And look at this." And the guy held up what looked like a pack of gum.

He just shrugged. He couldn't understand it. He couldn't believe it.

"Look," the guy said. "Look, *look*," and he bit his lip to hold back his excitement and laughter. "It's little hay," the guy said. "Little hay for little cows. Can you believe it? Can you make more sense than that?"

But he couldn't. He wanted to run, but he couldn't move. He just looked. "*But what do they do?*" he said, breathless.

The guy shrugged, put out his hands. "Moo, walk around," the guy said. "Look, when they die you can have a hamburger."

"They're cows," he said. He was quiet now. He was walking away. He knew the way back.

"Hey, wait a minute, buddy," the guy yelled to him. "Let's talk some business."

On the way back he stopped and looked in a store window but he didn't look in, just pointed his face that way. An older woman stood next to him. "You okay?" she said. He walked away. He put on his sunglasses. It had started raining. It smelled like rain and pavement. He went up the elevator and leaned on the elevator wall. He could barely get his key in the door. He would never come to New York City again. He felt dirty. He felt like he had sinned.

He rocked on his bed for awhile, his head in his hands. He felt gritty. Then he got up and looked out the window. He could hear thunder. It was really raining now. He could see people, cars. He could hear jackhammers, sirens, cows.

He could feel the water rising up.

NORTH CAROLINA

Cool

The kid across the street, he seems pretty cool. You've seen him sitting on the porch listening to country music on his boom box, looking into the boom box like it was TV. You think, maybe you and the kid have something in common. Maybe you could get to know each other.

Then one day you see a girl out in the yard with the kid. They are sitting on the lawn and they are kissing. You see that the girl is very beautiful—and you realize that the kid is very cool—and that you and the kid have nothing in common. That he has no reason to know you.

The Body

The moth came out of a pile of green two-by-fours. It was huge, maybe five or six inches wide and maybe three or four inches long. It was a light green. It had a fuzzy white body. It was one of the most beautiful things he had ever seen. And it made him sad that the moth was barely moving on the concrete floor, because it made him think of his girlfriend who loved all living things but didn't love him.

He wanted to show her the moth, have her hold the moth, take the moth away from the people who worked in the warehouse and nurse it back to health. He thought of showing the moth to the only gentle-looking girl in the warehouse. Show her: Look, isn't it beautiful?

But just then she came up to Mike and said: "Who'd you hear I was going out with? Do you think I'd be going out with some nigger? I'll work with niggers, I'll get along with niggers. Did you think I'd have a date with a nigger?"

So he told Mike: "Mike," he said, "Watch out for that moth there. Don't step on it."

Mike said: "Holy shit, ain't that some big ugly bug."

Eventually, Mike stepped on the moth while moving a fan, but didn't notice.

There was blue silvery stuff coming out of the body. He looked at the body all night. Finally, he threw the body behind the dumpster. It was too painful to look at. Besides, he wasn't paying attention to his work and with the nail gun accidentally nailed Mike's glove to the table with Mike's hand still in it.

The Dinners

I had a beer in the afternoon that made me sleepy. So I figured I'd take a half-hour nap, and then I was going to make dinner and watch the news, Connie Chung. I was going to spread spaghetti sauce on bread and then put tomatoes and green peppers and cheese on it. I was going to melt the cheese in the toaster oven.

But while I was sleeping I had this dream. All my old girlfriends were standing around my bed. They were all looking down at me. They were all beautiful. I was naked. They were all shaking their heads and mumbling.

"God, what were we thinking?" they were mumbling.

At one time or another I had made them all dinner. Some were good dinners and some were bad. They were all dinners.

That night I had dinner. But I skipped the bread. I spread spaghetti sauce on my hand and then put tomatoes and green peppers on my hand. Then I put cheese on my hand and melted it in the toaster oven.

Goldfish Bowl

The traffic was lousy. The people were stupid. What they had done was make a solid line of cars in the left lane. In the right lane was the slower traffic, maybe going the speed limit. The left lane was going about one mile over the speed limit.

Where I'm from you travel in the right lane and hop gingerly over to the left lane only to pass. I tried staying in the right lane, but what would happen was you'd get stuck, real fast, behind some old guy, and then you'd be stuck there all right, because it was almost impossible to get back into the left lane, the cars were so thick. I tried to hop back and forth, like you're supposed to. I tried to set an example: Look, you guys, see my signals, left lane, right lane, that's how you're supposed to do it.

But no one was listening.

Anyway, I'm over in the left, and I get behind this Pacer, that goldfish bowl of a car: round, fat, and all glass. There were two people in it, a guy and a girl. The girl was in the passenger seat. Her head just barely came over the top of the car seat, a teeny girl. But they had passed me earlier on and I knew that she was a normal girl, an adult girl, a girlfriend.

The guy looked pretty normal. I could see he had a mustache because he kept turning his head to the girl, looking right at her. His mustache sat there and his mouth would be moving. And it looked like he was yelling, yelling at the girl. Sometimes he would bash the headrest of her seat with his fist. Maybe he was talking, maybe they were just having a polite conversation. But it didn't look that way. It looked like yelling. And it didn't look like she was saying much of anything, although there were times when I could tell that he was waiting for her to answer some question he had posed. There were times when I could tell that he was waiting for an answer, losing more of his patience as every second went by. He would turn his head to her, wait, turn his head back to the road, turn his head back to her, and I could see him shout, "Well?" And he would slam his fist on the back of her headrest or the front dashboard. Sometimes the car would swerve a little, but not too bad.

In my head, I was piecing together his words, mostly phrases: *Am I right? I said, Am I right? I'm waiting for an answer. What could possibly be wrong with you? How stupid can you be?* I was starting to wonder the same thing. I was wondering what this teeny little girl could have possibly done that was so wrong that she was getting such a long and theatrical reprimand. I realized I'd been following this Pacer for almost forty-five minutes.

Still, the traffic was stupid. I had a long trip ahead of me. I looked over to the right and it looked like nobody was there, so I went, right, and zoomed past the traffic in the left, including the Pacer. As I went by I noticed the girl, she had her hands over her face.

Less than a minute later I came up behind an old white pickup doing around fifty. I waited until I saw the first semi-opening in the left lane and took it. It was in front of the Pacer. The guy was preoccupied, his mustache moving.

I caringly hit my turn signal and turned my wheel to the left. I could hear the Pacer behind me start to accelerate (bad muffler). The guy didn't want me in front of him, but it was too late, I was on my way. What was everyone doing in the left lane to begin with?

I looked in my rearview and I could see the guy. He had his hand up and was giving me the finger. He was slowly tapping it on his windshield, to more formally make his point. THE FINGER. THE FINGER. THE FINGER.

Spice Sandwich

He was writing a letter to his friend Steve when he realized that he hadn't eaten anything all day. There was an amazing electrical storm raging outside. No rain, just plenty of lightning, thunder, and wind, wind ripping and clattering his tin roof, blowing calendar pages off the walls. The thunder put the fear of god in him, but it was rain he needed, rain for the garden.

He went into the kitchen and checked in the refrigerator. There was nothing in there but an old carton of milk with a mess at the bottom. He looked at his cupboard and found a big line of ants going up to the cabinet door. He opened it and it was black with ants. The wind from the electrical storm blew some of them around and blew at his hair. Thunder shook the windows. The ants were in his Doritos and his spaghetti. They were in his package of cookies, which was empty. They didn't seem to have made it to the bread. He put all his food on the floor and sprayed a circle of Ant-Kill around it. He shook the ants out of his Doritos and waited for them to die. The wind kept blowing the bag out of the circle.

There were several ant lines on the floor and he sprayed them with Ant-Kill. There were ants on his legs and hands. He brushed them off. Rain began pounding the tin roof. It sounded like a B-52 was hovering on the roof.

A sandwich, he thought, and reached for his bread. Some ants were on it. He brushed them off. He looked for something to put on the bread. There was no lettuce, no peanut butter, no mayonnaise, no luncheon meat. My spices, he thought. They can't take that away from me. He brushed at the ants on his legs and face. He reached for his spices: garlic powder, red pepper, and oregano. Just then the force from a thunderclap shattered a kitchen window, sending ants and curtains sailing around the room. He had to hold the table for balance. It took a long time to get some spices on a piece of bread because they blew around so much. Finally, he got them there, brushed some ants off, and bit in. Rain was coming in all over now.

Spice sandwich, he thought.

It's good!

Bowl of Candy

After Rayvon died he came back
to my girlfriend in a dream.

"Here," he said. "So you will
remember me, I'm leaving this bowl
of candy for you on the coffee table."

"Each candy is a way to remember me.
This candy," he said, picking up a candy,
"is beer.
And this candy is my camper.
And this candy is my tractor."

"And this candy is the barbecue shack.
And this candy is my feet.
And this candy is my brother.
And this candy is more beer."

"When you feel sad," he said,
"just eat a candy."

The bowl will never get empty," he said, popping a piece of candy into his mouth.

Dolores

with enthusiasm

Dolores likes to stamp. Stamps everything twice, sometimes three times. Dolores is so enthusiastic that she breaks one of the stampers and I have to write APPR on each package with a marker. Dolores is a big fat woman. There's nothing particularly pretty about Dolores, but friendly, hell yes. Dolores is jolly, giddy. Dolores laughs at everything I say. Dolores likes this job, wrapping boards in paper, banding them and putting them in piles. Dolores says she can get me a job at Pallet Repair. That's where Dolores's old man works. They pay five dollars an hour there. Dolores would work there but they won't let women. Dolores pays $625 for her apartment. Dolores's old man tried to kill her and Dolores doesn't like that. Dolores wants to know if I've ever been anywhere. Dolores wants to go somewhere but she doesn't have a car. Dolores had a Subaru but she gave it to her old man. The bruises Dolores could show me. Dolores's old man picks her up in the Subaru when we get off at two a.m. Dolores's old man drives twenty-five miles per hour with the brights on the whole way. Dolores lives only a few minutes from my house. Dolores wants to know if I've ever been to the dances in Tyro. Dolores wants to know what kind of car I have. Country dances, Dolores says. Dolores says she is sad she won't see any of us until Monday. Dolores likes it here. Dolores is stamping me on my hand. Dolores is stamping everybody. Dolores wants to know if I can give her a ride home sometime. Dolores is laughing. Dolores has her hand on my shoulder. Dolores likes it here.

Dolores.

Dolores the big fat woman.

Hurrah!

Neanderthal

He was rummaging around, looking for some paper clips, when he found a box filled with some old love letters he had written and never sent, and some papers he had done for school. There were some pictures, too.

He read through the papers and love letters and realized that, all those years ago, his brain worked better. It seemed sluggish now.

He looked at the pictures. Somehow he looked, well, cleaner in the pictures. Leaner, less hairy.

He held the picture of himself up to the mirror and looked at himself in the mirror. His jaw seemed to jut out. He seemed stooped over. He had hair now where he didn't have hair before.

He went into the living room where his wife was reading *Architectural Digest*.

He grabbed her by the hair and dragged her, kicking and screaming, out into the yard, and then down into the woods.

He caught two rabbits with his bare hands, and they had a nice dinner.

We All Do Our Part

"Where's the phone," she said. She came up to Carlos all huffy-like, like she was in a hurry. Carlos didn't quite understand her. Carlos doesn't quite understand English, he just mops the floors. But he's a nice guy, always smiles.

"The phone," she said, blowing by Carlos, who was smiling.

She slapped her hand down on the desk. "Where is it?" She was just about yelling.

What a jerk, I thought. Bite my fucking head off. "It's over there," I pointed, taking my time. "Right near the soda machines."

She gave an exaggerated sigh, pushed off from the desk and went to the phones. No one should be so cranky to Carlos. Or to me. The girl was dressed in scruffy black clothes and wore a lot of makeup and cat's-eye eyeglasses. She was some sort of artist punky type. I mean, this is a nice hotel and she comes in bossing everyone around. I was hoping real hard she'd have to come back for some change.

Anyway, I smiled over to Carlos who smiled back to me and nodded. Then he looked in the direction of the phones, shook his head and went back to the floor.

I could see the girl over at the phone. She was asking for somebody and then she said, "No, I have to speak to him. I have to speak to him now." Then she put her head down and didn't say anything.

I looked back over to Carlos who was just mopping away and I heard this big sort of sob, sort of sigh come from where the girl was. Then she moaned, "noo," and leaned her head up against the telephone. She started crying and took off her glasses. "Lenny," she was saying. "Lenny, no. No."

And then I saw Carlos make his way over to the phones. He looked at the girl for a second, just watched her. Then, he set the CAUTION: WET FLOOR sign down about two feet in front of her, so that people would go around.

Dark

You've been living alone for so long that you realize that the neighbors across the street (you've never met them) are probably wondering about you, probably watching you. You think about this, about having your comings and goings monitored, being watched as you move around the yard, the house, from room to room (you have no curtains). How many times have they seen you come out of the bathroom in your underwear? How many times have they seen you dancing in the hallway?

You wait until it's pitch black outside, then you go out and pretend to check the mailbox. You want to see what kind of view they have.

But you see that your house, even lit up, looks dark.

HOLTON

He woke up with a start at six a.m. He did it again at six-thirty. It's my new job, he thought. First day.

Finally, seven came and he got up and made his lunch. He wondered if people made their lunch at his new job. Two peanut butter sandwiches. He couldn't find the right kind of bag to put them in so he had to put them both in one big paper shopping bag that said Winn-Dixie on it. The two sandwiches looked insignificant in such a big bag. He was ready for work.

He didn't know what his new job was, but he knew it was "something at the plastic works—light assembly." An agency was sending him. It was his first job for this agency: Dewdrop Temporaries.

He fixed his hair in his rearview mirror, put the key in the ignition and nothing happened, just *err, err, err.*

My car always works, he thought. It's never not worked. And today it doesn't work? He turned the key again, *err, err, err.*

My car always works, he thought. Something must've happened to my battery.

"Something's wrong with my battery," he told the lady from the agency.

"Don't worry," she said. "Just give us a call when you get it jumped."

Jumped, he thought.

He sat on his back porch. There was nobody who lived anywhere near him who loved him. He was new here. Most people, he thought, have already gone to work. How could he knock on somebody's door at this hour of the morning?

He tried to jump-start his car with the lawnmower, but the battery must not've been big enough. He put the lawnmower away. As he came out of the shed he heard a truck pulling out across the street.

Holton, he thought.

Holton owned the pig farm across the street. He had lots of trucks with big batteries.

But he had heard that Holton was a harsh man. He had heard that Holton had hit his father over the head with a beer bottle, making his father "not right."

"Holton," he said.

But Holton was already halfway down the road.

THE KID THAT EVEN THE DOGS DIDN'T LIKE

He ran from third and then slid into home. Dust flew up into the air. It was a good slide. He got up, brushed off his pants and did it again.

The game had been over for a half hour or so. All the kids and parents had gone home. He had watched the game from the edge of the woods, with the mosquitoes biting him.

He laid on the ground at home plate. He saw parents, coaches, and teammates above him. "Yes," the coach said. "You have won the game for us."

Then a big black dog came and chased him away.

RICE PUDDING

"Look," her mother said. "I made rice pudding."

"It is too vanilla-y," she said.

"Would you like some?" her mother said.

"I do not like the vanilla-like quality of your rice pudding," she said.

"I have one large bowl of rice pudding," her mother said. "And two small dishes. One for you and one for me."

"I must warn you this," she said. "I will have to chew gum in bed in order to get rid of the vanilla taste."

"Would you like some rice pudding?" her mother said.

"I will have a small dish," she said, fondling the gum in her pocket.

SPOT THAT MARK MADE

"I can't be trusted, Margo," Mark said. "Not with liquids, not with anything." She had given him grape juice before, countless times. But nothing like this had ever happened. Not to Mark, not to Margo.

Towels, Margo thought and got out of her chair. "Towels," she said.

"No, Margo," Mark said, getting up, putting his hands on her shoulders, pushing her gently back down into the chair. "I'll do it. It's paper towels we need. Paper towels and a wet sponge." He nodded, looking out the window. "This is one thing I can handle, Margo. This is one thing I can make right."

Margo had been pushed back into her chair. She had been pushed around by Mark before, and just like before she didn't say anything, didn't offer any resistance. "Mark," she should have said, "I know my own carpet. I can handle this spill." But she didn't. She just sat back in the chair, looking at the spot that Mark made.

It was grape juice, which was purple, but it made the carpet seem brown. The carpet was orange except for where the grape juice was, and there it was brown. It was a good brown. Margo crossed her legs and stared at the spot. What did it look like? It had a shape, but ... she didn't know. She could hear Mark bashing around in the kitchen, running water.

"These things happen, Margo," Mark said as he came back in, sponge and paper towels in hand. "I know what I've done. I admit it freely. And yes, I'm ashamed, Margo. I'm terribly ashamed. But these things happen, Pal. It happens to people all over the country. People are weak, Margo. Weak as hell."

"And I'm no different," he said. "I'm the weakest there is. We both know that. And we've been through this before and we've come out okay and we'll be okay again." He was on his knees wiping at the spot, blotting it with the paper towels and rubbing it with the sponge.

Margo sat there with her legs crossed. She was looking at the spot. She had her fingernail in her mouth, but she wasn't biting it. She was just stretching it out with her teeth.

Mark got off his knees with a groan. He cleared his throat.

"I don't know, Margo," he said, shaking his head at the spot. "That may be the best we get. That's maybe all I can do."

The spot wasn't gone, but it was more spread out. It was less defined now. But what was it?

Mark stood there looking at the spot like he was waiting for someone to say something but no one did. "Look," he said. This is what life is." He was looking her right in the eyes. He sold cars.

"I know we can handle this, Margo." His voice was getting quieter. "Together, Margo, we can work this thing out." And he reached down and touched her, put his arms on her sides like he was going to lift her out of the chair.

"Margo," he said.

But this time she put her arm out so it touched his chest and she extended her arm slowly so it pushed him away. He resisted, but not that much.

"Margo," he said. "It's just an accident, Margo. Something that happens between two people. Something that just happens." But Margo pushed him away and he stood up straight again.

"I'll get a steam cleaner, Margo. I'll make it just like it was." And he was out the door before she could tell him not to bother, before she could tell him that this carpet had had it. She didn't know if he had looked back or not. She just kept staring at the spot.

She could hear Mark's car starting out in the driveway, and then pulling out of the driveway.

She stared for just a few minutes trying to figure out what the spot looked like. But she couldn't think of anything, just a spot. Then she thought, *Wait, it looks like a duck.*

Then she went out and got in her car. She drove to the closest little twenty-four-hour place. (She didn't turn her radio on.) She went in and walked around for a minute as if she was just walking around. She looked at the ice cream and picked up a Leap Frog. But then she put it back down.

She bought grape juice, some frozen and some in bottles. She even bought some in little boxes. She just took as many as she could carry up to the counter and then went back for as many as she could carry. The girl at the cash register said: "Whoa."

When she got home she brought the grape juice into the house. She had bags full of grape juice. It took her three trips. She took a bottle out and opened it. It smelled like grape juice. She put the bottle to her lips. It had a wider mouth than a regular bottle. She took a sip and then filled her mouth with grape juice.

Now she was standing next to the chair with a mouth full of grape juice. She didn't feel like swallowing. She liked her mouth full. Then she swallowed.

She poured the rest of the bottle on the spot, which made the spot bigger and darker. It made a sound like a dog peeing on a carpet. The carpet was flooded with grape juice.

She thought that it looked like a cloud.

BAD, SUPERMAN, BAD

They both went to the office. They both came home.

It was later, and they were in bed. They had already made love.

"I've got to go out," he said.

"What?" she said.

"I've got to go out, Lois," he said. "I've got to save people. I've got to save them all."

"We've talked about this before," she said. "We hardly get to spend enough time together as it is."

"It's different now, Lois," he said. He sounded upset.

"I'm a superhero and a reporter," he said. "I never said I was anything else. I'm not a doctor and I'm not perfect, Lois. I make mistakes just like everyone else."

"It's okay," she said. "It's okay." But he was shaking. "Tell me, Clark. Tell me what it is."

"It was a few weeks ago," he said. "But God help me, Lois, it feels like yesterday. It feels like this morning. I was just out flying around, you know, just looking around. And I saw this old man crossing the street with this bag of groceries. It looked really heavy. And he fell. And there was this car coming, so I swooped down there, you know, in the nick of time and saved him.

"And all of these people came out of the shopping center. They always come out to see me save somebody. Why can't they just mind their own business?" He clenched his fists.

"Easy, hon," she said.

"Well, I figured the old guy had just tripped or slipped or something. But he didn't just fall. He was down on the pavement clutching his chest. And even I knew what was going on. Even a five-year-old could see he was having a heart attack. So like I said, Lois, I'm no goddamned doctor. I'm not." And he picked up a paperback and threw it right through the wall.

"C'mon, honey," she said. "C'mon." She was hugging him.

"So, I'm kneeling next to the guy. I'm just like everyone else now. 'Is there a doctor here?' I said. 'Is anybody a doctor?' But nobody was. Nobody knew CPR either. They were all just looking at me. 'You're Superman,' one of them says. 'You're Superman.' They kept saying it. Over and over. And they were right. Heaven help me, I am Superman. But what could I do? The guy is just moaning there.

"Finally, one of them says, 'Fly him to a hospital, you big fucking idiot.'

"What was I thinking, Lois? Why was I kneeling there, not knowing what to do?"

"It's okay," she said. "It's okay."

"It's not okay," he said. "It gets worse. I picked him up. I just scooped his little body up into the air with me."

"Good, Superman," she said.

"It's not good," he cried. "It's a hundred miles from good. It's as black as sin. I took the guy up. But I must've been pretty shaken. I must not've been thinking right. Because I couldn't find it, Lois. I flew all over the place, but I couldn't find the hospital."

"Okay," she said. "Okay." She was rocking him like a baby.

"So I landed on this hill. There was an apple tree, and I guess I tried to save him, like they do on TV. You've seen it. You do the thing on the guy's chest.

"But I'm Superman, dammit," he cried. "I pretty much just went right through the guy's chest. I didn't make his heart go. I didn't bring him back to life."

"Oh, my poor baby," she said.

"No, Lois," he said. "Not me. I guess I just went crazy after that. I thought about asking directions, about flying him to the hospital. But I knew they'd know. If he had just died. But I had crushed his chest. And all those people saw me fly away with him. I didn't know what to do. I couldn't just leave him there, could I?"

Then he calmed down a little bit and said: "So I just flew up with him, Lois. Up and up and up. All the way to the edge of space with this guy. This guy I had killed.

"Then I went into space with him. I let go of him and there we were, just the two of us floating there. I put my hand out and I touched him. I just touched him real lightly and his body floated over to the edge of the atmosphere and bounced back. He bounced back real soft like a balloon. It was so nice, Lois. So quiet and beautiful. I pushed him again and he did it again. I don't know how many times I did it.

"Then," he said, as his face went pale. "I pushed him through, Lois. I held him and pushed him through, back into the atmosphere. And he just took off. He fell so fast. I just watched him for awhile. Then I went down after him. And I caught up with him as he smoldered, started to burn. Skin, face, clothes, I.D., all burning as beautiful as a comet. I was laughing crazy then, but I'm not laughing now, am I, Lois?"

And he got up. And he stood in front of the bed, pulling his pajamas apart, revealing what was underneath. "That's why I have to go, Lois," he said. "Go and never come back. No one can ever die on Earth again. Not a dog, cat or any person. I have to save them all now, Lois. It's all I can do."

And he was out the window before she could tell him that it was okay. Before she could tell him that she still loved him.

BOWLING IN JERSEY

Linda had never bowled before. But she liked Chuck and so there she was. You had to give the big lady behind the counter one of your shoes or she wouldn't give you the bowling ones.

"Just one?" Linda asked.

"This ain't Russia," the lady answered. She handed Linda a pair of red-white-and-tan fives.

"What time do leagues start?" Chuck asked.

"Relax," the lady said. "You've got about four hours." She lit a cigarette and nodded. "You've got all day."

Linda put on her bowling shoes and carried her one remaining sneaker. Chuck carried his two bowling shoes and hobbled in his work boot down to where the balls were. Linda looked around, and Chuck said, "Don't be nervous." He put his arm around her.

"It's just all these people watching you," Linda said.

Chuck said, "They're only watching you to make sure you're not watching them."

There were racks of balls, mostly black. Chuck picked up balls, put them back down. He got a brown swirly one for Linda. "Try this," he said.

Linda put her fingers in the holes and held the ball down at her side. She thought, *I'm bowling*.

"How's that feel?" Chuck said.

"It feels good," Linda said. It felt heavy.

"Too heavy?" Chuck said.

"No, just right," Linda said. It was, after all, a bowling ball.

She did not really like the idea of bowling. It was something she did not think she would be any good at. But she did not tell

Chuck that she did not like the idea of it. When Chuck had called, Linda did not want to go. But then she said okay.

"We don't have to if you don't want to," Chuck had said.

"Okay," Linda had said again.

Some of Linda's friends had gotten married. Linda lived at home and worked at the drugstore and now she was going to bowl.

There were people in most of the lanes. It was pretty noisy with everyone cheering and yelling and the balls going down the lanes, hitting pins or not hitting pins. Chuck picked a lane. He sat down and wrote their names. He wrote *Chuck and Linda* on the score sheet. Linda sat down next to him, still holding her ball.

Chuck said, "Okay, you." But Linda did not want to go first.

Chuck got seven pins down and said, "Damn." He showed Linda where to write the seven. Then he got the rest of the pins down. He showed Linda how to make a sign for a spare.

Now it was Linda's turn.

"I don't know," she said.

"Sure you do," Chuck said, and patted her on the back.

She rolled the ball. It rolled into the gutter. It had trouble getting all the way down the lane.

Linda thought she was no good at bowling. She threw her next ball into the gutter, too. Chuck kissed her when she sat down, and said, "Come up here with me." He showed her how to hold the ball and where to put her feet and to put her arm back and stuff like that. But when he bowled, he got only three pins down.

In the first game, Chuck got one-twelve, and Linda got a forty-eight. The second game was something like that but better. Chuck two hundred, Linda ninety-one. Then they went and had pizza in the snack bar.

"You're doing good," Chuck said.

"Nnnn," Linda said.

"Real good," Chuck said. "Better than anyone I've been bowling with. Better than anybody. Swear to God." He held up his hand and shook his head. "Swear to God."

Chuck was a volunteer fireman.

I have bowled, Linda thought.

SALIVA

He sat in the movie house all by himself. He was watching a movie about a guy and a girl and a dog. They were traveling across Wyoming and meeting interesting people. There weren't that many people in the theater. But it wasn't like he had the place all to himself. Some people wouldn't see a movie by themselves. He knew some of those people. Seeing a movie was the same as watching TV, except that you go out so you don't feel as guilty.

"Karen," the guy on the screen was saying, "this is the most beautiful place I've ever seen." He looked like he meant it. He had his arm around Karen and a light breeze was blowing in their faces. Off to the side, you could see the dog scampering about in a field.

"Yes," Karen said. He knew that she was dying of cancer, but the movie guy didn't. The movie guy's name was Mal and he thought that they were just on a crazy spur-of-the-moment vacation.

They kissed, and you could see Karen's face, and she was crying because of the unfairness of it all and because of what a nice guy Mal was.

Oh, my God, he thought. *Poor Mal, poor Mal.* And then he thought, *Oh, God, poor Karen, too.* And he also thought about the unfairness of it all and how nice everybody was and how sad it is to die.

He didn't cry. He never cried. In fact, he had never cried since he was little. Except there was this one screwed-up time on *The Price Is Right*, where this nice old lady was going to win this whole vacation package and a pair of Honda motorcycles. For some reason, he thought how nice Bob Barker was and how happy the old lady would be and he got all choked up and cried.

But like I said, that was a screwed-up time.

He knew he wasn't going to cry, but he thought he might just get a little misty-eyed, a little choked up. He was choked up and they were kissing and she was crying. *Oh, man,* he thought. *Oh, Jesus,* and he started to choke up.

And then choke. Just a little saliva had gone down the wrong way. He tried to clear his throat with a very quiet, very polite little ahem, but it didn't work. He tried a little louder. "Ahem, mhm."

But it was to no avail.

On the screen, Karen had pushed Mal back and wiped away her tear. "Mal, I've got something to tell you," she said.

He coughed, just a quiet one, then a bit louder. *It's one of those things,* he thought. He was just going to have to keep coughing. "Ahem," he coughed. "Ahah aha ahem." He coughed, then tried to clear it out. "Mhmm mm. Mhmmm mm, mm, m. MHMMMM MMM! AHA AHA AHEM!"

"Shh," somebody behind him said.

"AHA AHEM!" he coughed.

Mal smiled. "You can tell me anything. You know that."

"AHA AHEM!" he coughed. He was really choking now.

"Take it outside, buddy!" someone yelled.

"AH HMMMNN!"

Now the whole place was yelling and shouting at him.

"What is it?" Mal asked. "What's the matter?"

The whole place was too busy yelling at him to hear it, though. They were making more noise than he was. He stood up, choking, and everybody started clapping. "LOOK, I'M JUST CHOKING ON SOME SALIVA, OKAY?" he gasped. "YOU DON'T HAVE TO BITE MY HEAD OFF! AHA AHEM!"

But nobody cared. They just wanted him out of the theater so they could see the rest of the movie.

"No," Karen said, looking away, the dog licking her hand, "this is serious."

BLINKY ASIAN KID

There he was on the train. He came in with his mom and his brother. He was the tiniest, but the way he was blinking and the Asian part made him seem older, wiser.

At first the three of them just stood there near the door. Then his mom looked around and found them some seats. There was a whole bunch of them, seats. The blinky Asian kid climbed up into the one she chose for him. His feet barely making it to the edge of the seat. His brother climbed up next to him, right in the very same seat.

The blinky Asian kid blinked and looked around, looked amazed. He put his hand out and pushed against the side of his brother. He didn't want his brother to sit in the same seat, not with so many other seats empty.

The blinky Asian kid was hardly done being an infant and yet he knew what space was.

And he looked over at me, amazed. Blink.

And I felt loved.

WAX PAPER

Last night I thought of wax paper. Actually, maybe I dreamed it, sat upright in bed and thought of wax paper. I thought, Where is it, what has become of it? What a great thing it was.

Someone thought of a wet fish and invented wax paper. What a good person. Wax paper was a concept, an idea.

I remember three kinds of sandwiches. Peanut butter and jelly, bologna with mayonnaise, and tuna fish. Those were my three sandwiches; they were all I ate. No cheese, no lettuce, no tomato.

I never traded sandwiches. A sandwich was made by my *mom*. She got up early and made it for me because she loved me. To give it away would be like saying, Thanks for the love, Mom, but I've got this over here.

I gave my apple away a lot.

Wax paper I don't remember enough about. Maybe it was because of Baggies. Baggies Alligator Bags with Twisties. I remember Paul Reilly and Ralph Scalise both had wax paper. Why? Baggies were newer, Baggies were better. They would keep what Mom made out of love tasting better. Much more like Mom had wanted it to be.

Oh yeah, egg salad, too. My mom would say, "You have to have Baggies for egg salad. Wax paper couldn't hold a candle to Baggies with egg salad."

But, still, wax paper. It was always in the house. My mom would use it for pies, for some reason I can't remember. Line the pie plate or something. And for something to do with cookies. I remember her saying, "Okay, get out the wax paper." And I knew right where the wax paper was. First drawer, silverware. Second drawer, bread. Third drawer, tin foil, Baggies Alligator Bags, and wax paper.

It makes me want to go back there. Not to say hi, not to see how things are, but to sneak in (I have a key) and check that third drawer and see if wax paper is still there.

NEW FORMAT

"Can I ask you something?" he said.

"What?" she said.

"Is there something funny going on?" he said. "Down there, I mean."

"Down where?" she said.

"Down there," he said. "In your crotch, I mean. Something, well, wrong or funny. I mean, why is my tongue all numb? Why is that?"

"I don't know," she said. "Maybe you were moving it too fast."

"Was it fast?" he said.

"It was fast," she said. "Hey, I know what that is," she said.

"Oh," he said.

"Spermicide," she said.

"Spermicide?" he said.

"Mm-hm," she said.

"Will all my teeth fall out or something?" he said.

"No," she said, "but all the germs in your mouth will die."

"So that's good," he said.

"Yes," she said, "that's good."

"I knew you were wetter than usual when you came in," he said. "I thought it was me. But it was just the spermicide."

"It was more than just the spermicide," she said. "But a lot of it was the spermicide."

"I thought I was a hot mama," he said.

"You're a hot mama," she said.

"Spermicide," he said, "and a diaphragm, and a prophylactic," he said.

"I'm sorry," she said.

"No, no," he said. "I like the spermicide. I like the diaphragm. I'm not crazy about the prophylactic, but I appreciate it. I'm glad it's there."

"Okay," she said.

"Can we get more up there?" he said. "Can we get a sponge and an IUD and some foam up there too?"

"No," she said. "All we can get is the diaphragm, the spermicide, and you."

"Okay," he said. "I like the diaphragm," he said. "It's like something less mysterious than the crotch itself. Something manmade. It's like having a McDonald's in every city."

"Uh-huh," she said.

Then they didn't say anything.

Then he said, "When I was younger I had this girlfriend. Actually, she wasn't my girlfriend. She was my best friend's girlfriend. My *best friend's*. But she still wanted to do it with me and I still wanted to do it with her. So we would do it."

"Uh-huh," she said.

"But we needed rubbers, and I was too scared to buy them. I was only sixteen."

"Mm-hm," she said.

"So I had her sneak up to his room, my best friend's room, and she would steal rubbers from her boyfriend to do it with me."

"Wow," she said.

"I wanted to have sex," he said.

"I understand," she said. "How's your tongue?"

"Still tingly," he said. "Maybe if you knew I was going to do that, with your crotch, I mean, maybe you could put that stuff in later on."

"How can I know if you're going to do that?" she said.

"I don't know," he said. "I never know what I'm going to do."

"Maybe you should just make sure you do that every night," she said.

"No," he said. "I don't want to do that every night. Maybe on Wednesdays and Fridays."

"What about Saturdays?" she said.

"No," he said. "I won't do it on Saturdays."

"Maybe you should get on the pill too," he said.

"I am on the pill," she said. "Maybe you should get a vasectomy."

"I got a vasectomy," he said.

"Oh," she said. "I used to use this other thing. It was a little tablet. You shove it up there and it dissolves."

"Wow," he said.

"But I only used it once. It said on the side of the box that it might cause a burning sensation."

"Holy cow," he said. "Did it?"

"Not to me," she said. "But him."

"Oh," he said.

"Just one more thing," she said.

"What," he said.

"It might be a cliché," she said.

"That's okay," he said.

"Hold me," she said.

Then they didn't say anything.

THE HAPPIEST GUY ON THE TRAIN

I didn't see him at first but I heard him. I thought it was kids running around the station, playing a game, yelling *EEE-EER* at one another, trying to keep each other from getting on the train in time. Then he jumped on real loud just as the doors were closing.

"EEE-ERR," he said. He was wringing his hands together, looking all over the train.

"Who's that?" someone on the train said.

"I don't know," someone else said.

The guy hopped up and down a little bit, then turned around and looked out the window. When the train started moving, he hopped up and down some more, said, "EEE-ERR," and looked out the window. He had his face so close to the window that it was getting all steamed up with his breath. I saw him try wiping the steam off with his hands, but I guess his hands were greasy, because the window kept getting messier.

"He's just making it worse on himself," this older woman said.

The guy was moving his head back and forth real fast as things went by out the window. "YOR-OR," he said. He was wringing his hands. Then he turned around and looked at everybody on the train. He scrunched his face up.

"Oh," this high school girl said, "he's afraid. Afraid of the train." People on the train nodded in agreement.

"It's just a shame," a man in a sweatsuit said.

The guy would hop up and down and make noise, wring his hands together, look at things out the window when they came by and then whirl around like a dancer and look everybody on the train up and down, scrunching up his face and making noise.

"Why is he looking at everybody?" the older woman asked.

"I don't know," said a man with a stroller. "But don't look right at him."

Everybody looked down. Everybody except for me. I felt like I wanted to help this guy. "He just wants you to look at him and smile," I said. "So he knows it's okay to be on the train." So I looked up, and the guy looked right at me with his face scrunched up, and I smiled. *It's okay to be on the train*, I smiled. *It's safe. There are friends here.*

"YEE-ERR," the guy said with gusto and started heading down the aisle.

"Nice going," the man with the sweatsuit said. "He's going to come over and fog your whole face up now."

"Oh, man," the high-school girl said.

"YOREE-ERR," the guy said, but went on past me. He ran down the aisle, making noise and jumping up and down. He looked out both sides of the train, wrung his hands together. He ran back to the door, jumped up and down.

"Wait a minute," the man with the sweatsuit said, "he's not afraid of the train. He loves the train."

"He thinks the train is great," the high-school girl said.

"It's a lot of fun for him," I said.

"He wants you to share his joy," the woman said.

"But don't look directly at him," the man with the stroller said. And nobody did.

RICE KRISPIES AND BANANAS

He didn't think he wanted to get up but he did. He went downstairs and felt dirty sitting at the kitchen table in his bathrobe. He thought about the shower and he thought about breakfast.

He put the Rice Krispies in a bowl and put milk and sugar on the Rice Krispies. He waited for them to make noise. He cut up a banana with a knife that had ridges on it. He sliced his finger. Blood came out but it didn't hurt. He liked it. Must be a sharp knife, he thought.

He cut both his wrists open with the knife and then stuck his wrists into the bowl of cool Rice Krispies. He laid his head down on the table.

Aw, wait a minute, he thought, *there's crumbs on this table.*

THE RESTAURANT OF THE THIRD EYE

I dreamed I was in a diner or a B movie.
There was this older woman who comes in every day,
has lunch until late afternoon.

Then there was the B movie part. Two guys in
cotton shirts and Bert Convy haircuts grow an
extra eye in the middle of their foreheads.

First one guy does it and then the next.
They're sharing a table and they're buddies.
The first guy does it and then starts screaming like

maybe his brain has gone bad along with the eye thing.
The first guy starts smashing up the place and the second
guy just looks real terrified. Then he does it, too.

Everyone in the restaurant screams and runs over each other
trying to get out.
Except for the old lady who says,
"Again, but less ice this time.
Let's see if we can get this one a little crisper."

And she holds up
her glass which I guess
is a Manhattan.

BLIND ASIAN WOMAN WITH DOG

The chemist sat at his desk working out formulas on paper. He didn't have his own office; instead, he had his own desk in a room with miles of desks: people in lab coats, working out formulas on paper.

This was the Ideas Rendering Department. Here, people at miles of desks thought things up, things that could be made into things.

The idea of the miles-of-desks thing was to get people to gather, fool around, throw around ideas, be creative. But mostly these were just simple chemists, and even though there were miles of desks, hardly anyone talked to anyone else. They just worked things out on paper, drank coffee, or went to other departments to talk about materials, costs, etc. About how things on paper become things.

The first day the chemist saw the blind Asian woman was a few weeks ago, a Tuesday. He had left Ideas Rendering to go down to Packaging Implants to confer about something. If you think his office was big, you should see the whole plant. Miles upon miles upon MILES of hallways, all looking just the same, except for a colored stripe indicating which hallway, which area you were in. Because there were so many hallways, they not only had to have stripes but names. The hallways were named after presidents. And because the hallways were miles and miles long, the chemists, etc., couldn't walk from one end to the other, so the company provided scooters.

He was on a scooter going down the Millard Fillmore when he first saw her. She wasn't on a scooter because she was blind. She just came whipping around the corner, led by her dog, who was a seeing-eye dog but was running to beat the band.

Usually when you see a blind person with a dog, both of them are walking very slowly and looking very serious. But this woman and this dog were running like crazy, with big smiles on their faces. She had a red hooded windbreaker on and a backpack. The dog had a big tongue and a seeing-eye-dog harness. They looked like the two happiest creatures alive.

They ran right past him and around the corner toward the John Quincy Adams.

He stopped his scooter and looked at the corner. They were gone. They were gone before he could take it in. Then he took it in, but it was too late. The chemist was just standing in the hallway. The Millard Fillmore had a purple stripe.

The rest of his day went okay. The chemist rode on scooters, hung out in Packaging Implants, and had a tuna-fish sandwich. He went home and watched a TV show about a girl dying of cancer. Then he went to bed.

He had his own apartment with a bedroom with walls.

He thought he would go to sleep, but instead he thought about the blind woman. He thought of removing her backpack and red windbreaker. The two of them were naked and making love. The dog was sitting at the side of the bed, looking intense, then panting happily and rolling over as the chemist and the blind woman had their orgasms.

A few days went by. At night, the chemist would think of the blind woman. Sometimes they rode around in cabs. During the day, he would invent things on paper, go to Materials Configuration or Supplies Invoicing or Chemicals Categorization or Packaging Implants.

One day, he was riding a scooter from Ideas Rendering to Ideas Rendered with an idea. He was in the Abraham Lincoln and around the corner came the blind woman and her dog. She looked exactly the same. The Abraham Lincoln was long and straight, with a maroon stripe. He got to see her from a long way back, and he got to watch her run all the way. He smiled, but she didn't notice because she couldn't see.

He just stood there and listened to her footsteps and the dog's toenails as they faded away. He looked at his watch. It was 10:45.

Another chemist came scooting by. "Chemist, you're just standing there," the other chemist said. And then he went to Ideas Rendering.

From then on, the chemist went and stood in the Abraham Lincoln every day at 10:45. The first day, she didn't show up. The second day, she did. Then the third day she did, but the fourth day she didn't. Then it was the weekend.

He went home and thought about the two of them sitting on a park bench, kissing. He hoped he could make her as happy as running down the hallways did.

He wanted to lie in the hallway across their path. He wanted her and the dog to trip over him, her falling right onto his chest. He wanted to say, "I'm smiling at you."

Then one day, he got a progress report from Products Realization. A suds he had invented cleaned better than any other suds. He got a big bonus in the mail. He saw her that day and he wanted to tell her. As she went by, he got up his courage. "I made a suds," he said. But over the noise of the woman and of the dog panting, and of footsteps and of toenails, the chemist realized he hadn't said it loud enough.

The next day, there was a notice on his desk. It said his suds was a success and he was being promoted. He was going to Master Concepts, in Washington, D.C.

He stood in the Abraham Lincoln that day, but the blind woman didn't show up. A lot of chemists went by.

He went back to his desk and put his things in a box. Nobody said goodbye to him. He didn't think anyone knew he was leaving.

He picked up a formula for a sponge he was working on, a sponge he would take to Master Concepts, in Washington D.C.

But he realized that he didn't want to invent a sponge. He wanted to invent eyes. He wanted to invent a picture of himself in Braille, smiling.

NEW BALTIMORE SERVICE AREA

He pulled over because he was getting a little tired and he thought he might go to the bathroom, maybe get a candy bar and a Coke.

In the bathroom there was a guy, a janitor-type guy. The janitor guy was doing the sinks, one and then another—a little guy, maybe retarded. The janitor guy looked up from the sink he was doing and smiled: *Hi*.

He smiled back at the janitor guy: *I appreciate what you're doing*.

He went to a urinal, a medium one. There were the kiddie ones and then, I don't know, teenage ones, and grown-up ones. He figured he was at a teenage one. It was nice to have different sizes. He looked down, the strong deodorizer and little sneaker prints on the sides: a father holding his little son up to pee. A wonderful image filled with love.

The janitor guy had finished only one sink, the kiddie one. That's where he went, to the clean sink, with a smile: *I'll use the one you cleaned because you did such a good job*.

A look back: *That's the kiddie sink*.

Okay, so maybe the janitor guy doesn't understand, it's the gesture that counts.

He washed his hands and then leaned way down to wash his face. When he straightened up, there was a face right up in his face. It was the janitor guy's.

"What about the little children?" the janitor guy said. "Where will they go? Where will they go to wash?"

He smiled at the janitor guy. "I don't know," he said.

He didn't know.

He didn't know about the little children.

FLASH CARDS

I am holding up a series of flash cards in front of my cat.

"Do you recognize this one?"

Nothing.

"No? How about this one?"

Nothing, although, he's not ignoring me, which he sometimes does. "Well, how about this one?" I am trying to hide my annoyance, but doing a poor job of it. People say that animals cannot learn much—but how can we know their true potential if we do not even try?

"What about this one? This one's easy," I say.

Nothing.

I am reaching a frustration point and will have to quit in a minute. I am acting like I have shown him these cards a hundred times before. Which, it being about a third of the way into the year, and since I got these for him as a Christmas present, it is probably true. But this is illogical thinking on my part. I'm holding them up as if he recognized them at one point to begin with. As if this was just review, which it is not. Review is what flash cards are all about. But I know, deep down, that he never even recognized one of these cards in the first place.

Now, just a couple more cards.

CORK

If you are like us you are probably up in arms at the moment at the news that you cannot recycle cork.

Our building and outside in the streets—the whole neighborhood is going crazy. Upstairs, behind closed windows, families with older men and ladies are gnashing their teeth. Garments rendered. In other places, one street over, things are being thrown while others are being tipped over.

In still others, nothing is being said and nobody is moving a muscle but you can cut the tension with a knife. Mostly it is mayhem. Windows being broken, glass all over the street. Traffic has come to a standstill. Thank god, someone has the presence of mind to write a letter—but stops halfway through when she realizes she has no idea whom to send it to.

Wait. Someone just looked it up on the Internet. Turns out you can recycle cork, but it is a very difficult and inconvenient process. There is a moment of thoughtful silence, and we are up in arms again.

PROTEST

A protest came through my apartment this morning. I heard them crash through the door and march down the hallway with their slogans and placards and their bullhorn, chanting call and responses that you couldn't understand.

They marched up to me where I was sitting at my desk in my underwear reading the paper and enjoying my morning coffee, and threw a small bucket of red paint on me.

"Stop wearing fur," one of them said. "This is the blood of animals on you."

"But I do not wear fur," I said.

They started chanting unrecognizable things: *What do we want? Something. When do we want it? Sometime.* The chant got louder and faster until it fell apart altogether with a congratulatory *woo*, and then there was general silence.

They pulled a few of the books from my bookshelves. They knocked over my lamp. They mussed up the blankets and pillows on my bed. They frightened my cat. Most of them just milled about and commented under their breath about the unkemptness of my apartment.

"What? You can't do a dish?" I heard one of them say clearly from the kitchen.

Most of them, however, just stood fairly still, shuffling from one foot to the next, looking either up or down. They did not know what, really, they were supposed to do in such cramped quarters. I do not believe they had okayed their route ahead of time with the local officials. There was simply no room left in my apartment. They had filled up the living room and down the hall, solid. I assume that the kitchen was full as well. A small, indecipherable, displeased-with-the-state-of-things rumble filled the rooms. Who knows what was going on in my bathroom?

Red paint/blood was all in my coffee. It dripped down my head into my face and soaked my underwear with its cold stickiness. It dripped in my right eye and made it twitch, sting, and blink uncontrollably. I did not know where to rest my dripping hands.

Someone picked up my coffee mug and threw it through the front window. The shattering was very loud and impressive.

"We're on the third floor," I said to the thrower. "What if that hits somebody?"

The thrower said nothing, just looked down at the floor as if it never happened.

The one with the bullhorn, the lady, I believe, who was leading the charge, gave me a sideways glance and said conspiratorially: "I'm very sorry about this. This was supposed to have been a nonviolent protest, just the marching and the bullhorn, the slogans and the bucket of blood. But, you know how it is," she said.

I did know how it was, and I said as much.

PEPPER

It wasn't until I began sneezing that I noticed I smelled pepper. It was the guy sitting right in front of me at the cafe, his back to me, his beautiful wife sitting directly across from him. They were laughing and being in love and they were having their coffee and their morning together, before going to their jobs in their his-and-hers BMWs, where they both laugh and laugh and have fun all day long before coming home, traffic-free, each to a loving and understanding partner.

The door to the cafe was open and a breeze was coming in. And his bagel, having just been peppered, was waiting to be placed in his delightful mouth, ground by his pearly-white teeth, caressed through his wonderful esophagus and then to rest gently in his perfect stomach. But that pepper, borne on the cool breeze, had sent me into a sneezing fit of eight to ten sneezes. I never sneeze only once. God, in that way, did not bless me. And now snot and saliva was escaping my head. I had to grab for a napkin. I had to interrupt my work. The guy had won this round, and every round before that and after that.

BEVERAGE DISPLAY CASE

On his way to take a leak in the bathroom of the coffeeshop, he passed the soda machine. Not a machine; one of those industrially lit, glass-doored refrigerated display cases that highlight the attractive cans and bottles he used to love so well, the peppy logos and the beautiful, luminescent liquids inside.

And as he passed, not even turning his head or looking, just thinking about his impending leak, he thought he heard the voice of his old girlfriend; a quiet call from the interior of the beverage display case. "Billy."

He didn't turn, or stop, or look at the sodas; he simply moved into the bathroom, so tiny, but well maintained, a blessing, really, considering the condition of most public bathrooms. And as he unzipped and went, he realized what he thought he had heard. Did I just hear Malminia call my name? Wasn't that Malminia's voice, calling "Billy"? Not calling, just saying it, just simply saying my name as she saw me pass the soda case: "Billy."

After all, didn't Malminia live, for ten years, in the apartments directly behind the coffeeshop? Didn't she hate me for ten years, and never once talk to me, or look at me for those ten years, even though we spent hours and hours and hours so together and so completely separate there in the tiny, tiny little coffeeshop, sometimes no more than a table between us, and the knotted tension of the shared memory of the terrible demise of our completely flawed relationship?

And wouldn't there be some sort of odd logic in the possibility that she, somehow, during her move from the neighborhood, came in for one last coffee and somehow got swept or sucked into the display case, somehow got hung up in the soda display, perhaps injured, too weak to speak for these last few years, surviving off the sodas and the juices, and the juice blends in the soda case? Waiting for her strength to return, so that she could call out for help. Her new fiancé, all this time, standing in their new-mown yard, waiting for her to show up at the new house he had built for them. *A dream house.*

And wouldn't the sight of Billy, the horrible boyfriend she barely ever even had, but hated so much that she wouldn't so much as look at him for ten years after, be enough to boost her adrenaline to speak, perhaps for the first time in two years: "Billy."

And perhaps it wasn't a cry for help at all. It didn't sound like one. Perhaps she had just wanted someone to know that she lived in the beverage display case now, had found a place to finally call her own, where she wouldn't have to speak, or listen, or look at anyone for the rest of her life. As chilly as her new surroundings were, they suited her personality to a T.

But, Billy thought, this was very likely craziness. A kind of crazy logic he had spent much of his adult life keeping at bay. It did not, he remembered, make sense for a woman to live in a soda-display case, no matter what her personality was like.

And so, as he left the bathroom and shut the door, he felt he had shut the door on craziness and nonsense. He did not even turn his head to see the soda case, whether she was all tangled in there, waving feebly or not.

Besides, she was the crazy one, not him.